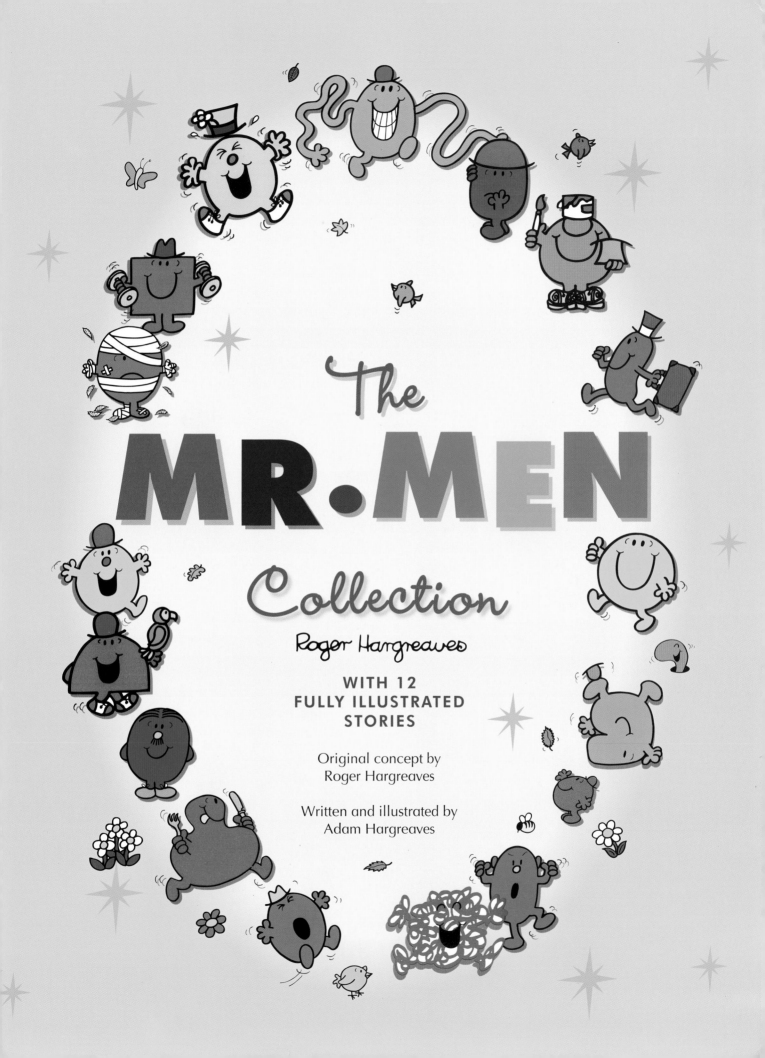

The
MR·MEN
Collection

Roger Hargreaves

**WITH 12
FULLY ILLUSTRATED
STORIES**

Original concept by
Roger Hargreaves

Written and illustrated by
Adam Hargreaves

MR. MEN   **LITTLE MISS**

MR. MEN™ LITTLE MISS™ © THOIP (a Sanrio company)

Mr. Men Collection © 2014 THOIP (a Sanrio company)
Printed and published under licence from Price Stern Sloan, Inc., Los Angeles
This edition published in Great Britain 2014 by Egmont UK Limited,
The Yellow Building, 1 Nicholas Road, London W11 4AN

ISBN 978 0 6035 7059 9
59158/1
Printed in China

CONTENTS

MR.
TICKLE
and the Dragon

Roger Hargreaves

Mr Tickle was having a very good day. Twenty one people well and truly tickled. A very good day indeed.

But when he arrived home, he could not believe his eyes.

"I can't believe my eyes," he said to himself. "Somebody has burnt down my house!"

Mr Tickle's house was gone. All that was left was a smoking, charred pile at the end of his garden path.

There was more smoke rising from the end of the lane.

Mr Tickle set off to investigate.

The smoke was coming from Mr Funny's shoe car. Or rather, it had been his car, but all that remained was a burnt shoelace.

Mr Tickle could see another spiral of smoke in the distance.

This time it was Mr Clever's house, and very nearly Mr Clever by the look of him!

"I just got out in time," said Mr Clever. "There can only be one culprit. It must have been a ..."

But Mr Tickle did not wait to hear what it must have been. He had spotted the signs of another fire and was determined to follow the trail.

It was a long trail which led from Mr Chatterbox's burnt out phone box to Farmer Field's burnt down barn, and on through wilder, bleaker land, up into the mountains. Soon it began to get dark, but Mr Tickle continued to climb higher and higher.

Darkness had fallen when he saw a bright light.
In the distance, there was a cave emitting a red glow.

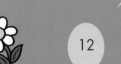 

Suddenly Mr Tickle did not feel very brave. Suddenly he wished he had stayed to hear what Mr Clever had to say.

Mr Tickle decided to wait there until the morning. He curled up under a bush and wrapped his arms around himself three times to keep warm.

Mr Tickle fell into a surprisingly deep sleep and the sun was up when he was woken by the rustling of the bush.

Mr Tickle opened an eye.

The bush rustled again.

"I know you're in there," rumbled a very deep voice. "Come on! Show yourself!"

Mr Tickle cautiously poked his head through the top of the bush and stood blinking in the bright sunlight. He was quite unprepared for the sight that met his eyes.

He was standing face to face with a dragon!

A huge dragon at that.

A huge dragon with smoke curling from his nostrils.

Mr Tickle gulped.

"Hello," said Mr Tickle, in a tiny voice.

"I'm going to give you thirty seconds to give me a good reason why I shouldn't burn you to a crisp," bellowed the dragon, "and then I'm going to burn you to a crisp!"

Mr Tickle gulped for the second time.

Mr Tickle needed to think fast. He realised his arms were hidden. Quick as a flash he sent one of his extraordinarily long arms snaking through the bushes and under the Dragon's belly.

Mr Tickle flexed his fingers and hoped beyond everything that dragons are ticklish.

The Dragon instantly crumbled into a giggling, laughing tangle on the ground.

"Ha! Ha! Ha!" roared the Dragon.
"Hee! Hee! Hee!" wheezed the Dragon.
"Ho! Ho! Ho!" boomed the Dragon.
"Stop it! Stop it!" he cried.

"I'll stop tickling if you promise to stop burning things," said Mr Tickle.

"Anything! I'll promise anything!" pleaded the Dragon.

Mr Tickle stopped tickling and looked the Dragon squarely in the eye.

"What you need to learn," said Mr Tickle, "is to put your fire breathing to good use. You should be using your extraordinary skills to make people happy. I'll show you."

The Dragon lay down on the ground and Mr Tickle hopped on his back. Then the Dragon shook out his great wings and took off, circling high over the mountains and swooping down to the distant valleys.

They flew lower and lower, passing over barns and cottages.

"Look!" cried Mr Tickle. "It's Little Miss Splendid's house. I have an idea for your first good deed!"

Mr Tickle and the Dragon stood beside Little Miss Splendid's swimming pool.

"It is too cold today to swim in Little Miss Splendid's pool," said Mr Tickle. "Do you think you could do anything about that?"

The Dragon thought for a moment.

Then he took a deep breath and breathed out through his nostrils. Flames licked across the surface of the swimming pool. In no time at all the pool was steaming.

Little Miss Splendid was delighted. Mr Tickle, the Dragon and Little Miss Splendid had a very enjoyable swim.

In fact, the Dragon had a very enjoyable day.

He melted the ice on Mr Bump's path, and Mr Bump couldn't have been happier, as most mornings he usually slipped up and bumped his head.

He warmed up Mr Forgetful's cup of tea which he had made at breakfast time and forgotten to drink. Mr Forgetful was delighted. He doesn't normally get to drink hot tea!

And Mr Greedy was very impressed when the Dragon cooked fifteen sausages all at once.

By the end of the day, the Dragon had a big glowing smile across his face.

"Do you know what?" he boomed, cheerfully.
"I feel really good!"

Mr Tickle grinned and then he reached out his extraordinarily long arms

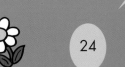

… and tickled the Dragon!

"And now I do too!" he laughed.

MR. NOSEY
and the Beanstalk

Roger Hargreaves

Mr Nosey is one of those people who is curious about everything.

If he comes across a parcel he will start to wonder what's inside it.

And the more curious he becomes the more he has to know.

And even if it is addressed to someone else, Mr Nosey will not be able to stop himself opening it.

Just to have a look.

His curiosity always gets the better of him.

One day, Mr Nosey was out for a walk when he met a Wizard. The Wizard was holding a small bag.

Mr Nosey, being Mr Nosey, had to know what was inside the bag.

The Wizard told him that it was a bag full of magic beans.

Mr Nosey had to know what was magic about them.

"I will give you one bean," said the Wizard. "And if you take it home and plant it, you will find out. That is, if you're sure that you want to find out."

What a silly question. Of course Mr Nosey was sure he wanted to find out!

At home, Mr Nosey planted the bean in his garden. The next morning he could not believe his eyes.

There in the middle of his garden was a giant beanstalk that stretched up into the clouds.

As Mr Nosey admired the beanstalk a thought occurred to him.

"What could be at the top of the beanstalk?"

The more he thought this thought, the more curious he became, and the more curious he became, the more he had to know.

So he began to climb the beanstalk.

He climbed …

… and he climbed …

… and he climbed. Right up into the clouds.
And when he reached the top he could not believe his eyes.
(For the second time that day.) There in the clouds was a giant castle!

And then a thought occurred to him.

"Who might live in a castle in the clouds?"

And the thought grew into curiosity, and the curiosity got the better of him. So he set out across the clouds to the castle.

The giant castle had a giant door, and in the giant door there was a giant keyhole.

Mr Nosey cannot pass a keyhole and resist the urge to have a peek, and this time was no different.

Except that this time it was different because Mr Nosey could fit through the keyhole.

Once inside, it quickly became apparent that the 'who' who lived in the castle was a giant.

Now you or I would have sensibly left as fast as we could.

In fact, we would not have been there in the first place. But Mr Nosey, as you can guess, could not resist having a look around.

Mr Nosey went into the Giant's kitchen and in the corner were three small cupboards. Of course Mr Nosey had to know what was inside them.

He opened the first cupboard. Inside was a small bag.

Before he could look inside the bag he heard a terrifying sound.

THUMP!

THUMP!

THUMP!

It was the thud of the Giant's heavy-booted footsteps, somewhere in the castle, and they were getting closer.

Mr Nosey grabbed the bag, scrambled through the keyhole and slithered back down the beanstalk as fast as he could.

Safely back at home he discovered that the bag was full of gold coins!

That night he could not sleep. He lay in bed thinking about the other two cupboards.

"What could they contain?"

He just had to know.

Early the next morning back up the beanstalk went Mr Nosey, back through the keyhole and back to the second cupboard in the Giant's kitchen.

Inside it was a hen.

"That's curious," thought Mr Nosey to himself, not for the first time in this story!

He picked up the hen and there was a golden egg.

"A hen that lays golden eggs," murmured Mr Nosey. "I'll need to take this home for a closer look."

Just then Mr Nosey heard the heavy boots of the Giant coming down the stairs.

THUMP!

THUMP!

THUMP!

Mr Nosey tucked the hen under his arm and ran for his life.

The hen fascinated Mr Nosey, but it did not stop him thinking about the third cupboard. He was terrified of the Giant, but his curiosity overcame his fear and so, the following morning, back to the Giant's kitchen he went.

He opened the third cupboard and in it was a golden harp.

A golden harp that was singing!

Mr Nosey sat and listened to the harp. He felt safe, knowing that he would be able to hear the Giant's loud boots coming.

But the Giant was wearing his slippers that morning, which is how he caught Mr Nosey.

"So you're the thief!" boomed the Giant. "I have a mind to grind your bones to make my bread!"

Mr Nosey's eyes nearly popped out of his head.

"But I won't," continued the Giant. "I prefer cornflakes for breakfast. Now, I know what to do with you. Since you are so interested in what is in my cupboards, you can clean them out for me."

And Mr Nosey did.

It took him three whole days.

Giant's cupboards are … well, giant.

"Now let that be a lesson to you," said the Giant.

And you'd think it would have been, but the very next day Mr Nosey came upon an empty house and the front door was open and on the kitchen table were three bowls of porridge …

… but that's another story.

MR. JELLY
and the Pirates

Roger Hargreaves

Mr Jelly is the most nervous person you will ever meet. The slightest thing will send him into a panic.

Even the sound of the wind in the trees will make him bolt behind the sofa, quivering and shaking in fear.

So as you can imagine, it takes Mr Jelly a long time to pluck up enough courage to go on holiday.

This year, Mr Jelly went to Seatown.

Mr Jelly longed to join everyone playing in the sea, but he was too frightened.

"Why don't you go for a swim?" suggested Mr Lazy.

"I … I'm too scared," admitted Mr Jelly. "There might be nasty seaweed … or a crab … or … or a shark!"

"Well, why don't you go out in my dinghy?" replied Mr Lazy.

"I … I … might drift out to sea and never be found again," said Mr Jelly, trembling at the thought.

"No you won't," said Mr Lazy. "Not if I hold on to the rope."

Mr Jelly thought this over and decided to risk it.

After a while, Mr Jelly began to enjoy himself in the dinghy. But when he looked back, he discovered that he was a very long way from the beach.

Mr Lazy had fallen asleep and the rope had slipped through his fingers!

"Oh help! Oh help! A wave is going to turn over the boat and I'm going to be swallowed by a whale!" shrieked Mr Jelly. But he was too far away for anyone to hear him.

Before long the land disappeared and large, black storm clouds gathered on the horizon.

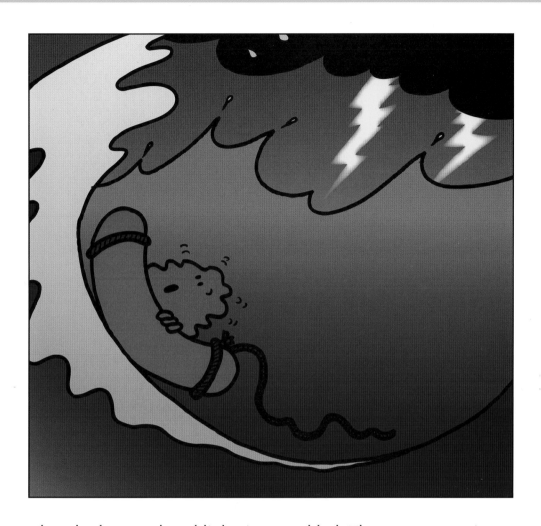

Thunder boomed and lightning crackled. The sea rose up in a great roaring mass that tossed the little dinghy from wave to wave.

Mr Jelly cowered in the bottom of the boat.

"Oh help! Oh help!" he shrieked. "I'm going to be struck by lightning, and burnt to a crisp, and tipped out of the boat and drowned!"

And then he fainted.

When he came to, he discovered that he had been washed up on to a tiny, deserted island.

Mr Jelly stared out at the vast expanse of sea.

"Oh help," he said in a very small voice, and then he fainted again.

Mr Jelly was woken by the sound of digging. He peered through the bushes at the side of the beach. What he saw filled him with terror …

Three swashbuckling, ruthless-looking pirates were digging up a treasure chest!

Mr Jelly knew that he must not make a sound, but the more he tried not to make a sound, the more he wobbled and trembled in fear. And the more he wobbled and trembled, the more the bushes shook and rustled.

So, in a very short time, Mr Jelly was found and set, quivering, on the sand in front of the pirates.

"Well, shiver my timbers, if he ain't just what we need," growled the pirate Captain. "A cabin boy!"

The three pirates and their new cabin boy rowed out to their ship, anchored in the bay.

Mr Jelly shook and trembled and quivered in terror.

The pirates, who prided themselves on their bravery, chuckled and laughed. They had never met anyone as nervous as Mr Jelly.

And over the following week, they came to realise just how nervous Mr Jelly really was.

On the first day, the first mate ordered Mr Jelly up into the rigging to set the sail.

"Oh help! Oh help!" shrieked Mr Jelly. "It's so high up and I'm going to have to climb and climb, and then I'll be even higher up, and I'll get dizzy, and I'll fall down into the sea and I'll be eaten by a shark!"

And then he fainted.

Luckily he had only climbed two rungs and the first mate caught him easily.

"I'd never thought of that," murmured the first mate to himself.

The next day, the quartermaster ordered Mr Jelly to sharpen the cutlasses on the grinding stone.

"Oh help! Oh help!" shrieked Mr Jelly. "I'll make the cutlass very sharp, and it will be so sharp that I will cut my finger, and then I'll bleed and bleed and …"

And then he fainted.

"I'd never thought of that," mumbled the quartermaster to himself.

On the third day, the gunner ordered Mr Jelly to practise firing the cannon.

"Oh help! Oh help!" shrieked Mr Jelly. "I'll load the cannon, and then fire the cannon and the explosion will be so loud that I'll go deaf, and then I won't be able to hear anything, and then …"

And then … well, you know what happened then.

He fainted.

Again.

"I'd never thought of that," muttered the gunner to himself.

And so it continued all week.

Mr Jelly even fainted when the cook ordered him to light the stove in the galley because he was afraid he would set the ship on fire!

And a very strange thing happened during the week. Not only did the pirates discover how nervous Mr Jelly was, but they also began to find out how nervous they were, too.

The more Mr Jelly shrieked and fainted and quivered and quaked at what terrible accidents might happen, the more the pirates found themselves worrying. By the end of the week, the pirate Captain found himself with a crew who were too scared to do anything.

Even the ship's carpenter had downed tools because he was afraid he might get a splinter!

"This is hopeless!" roared the Captain. "How can we call ourselves pirates? That cabin boy has turned you all into scaredy cats. Mr Jelly must walk the plank!"

So, Mr Jelly was pushed out on to the plank.

"Oh help! Oh help!" shrieked Mr Jelly. "Don't make me walk the plank. I'll fall into the sea and then I'll have to swim for hours and hours and then I'll get weaker and weaker and then I'll drown!"

"That's horrible," said the first mate.

"Yeh, really nasty," agreed the quartermaster.

"We can't do that," said the gunner.

And the rest of the crew agreed.

"That's it!" cried the Captain. "I give up. Do what you want!"

And the crew did.

They sailed, very cautiously and very slowly, to Seatown, where they let Mr Jelly off.

Mr Jelly found Mr Lazy on the beach.

Fast asleep.

Mr Lazy yawned, stretched and opened an eye. "Hello," he said, sleepily. "Did you have fun? Sorry I fell asleep, but here you are safe and sound."

Mr Jelly began to wobble and quiver and shake.

But not in fear.

Mr Jelly was very, very, very angry!

MR. GREEDY
and the Gingerbread Man

Roger Hargreaves

It was not long after he'd finished his breakfast that
Mr Greedy started to feel hungry again.

He had eaten three packets of cornflakes, two loaves of bread
and one pot of jam, but Mr Greedy's tummy was telling him
that it was feeling peckish.

"What to have?" thought Mr Greedy to himself.

"I know," he said out loud.

"I shall make a gingerbread man."

And because he is Mr Greedy, he made an extra large gingerbread man, which he put in the oven.

And while he was waiting for it to bake, he had a snack.

A chocolate biscuit.

Followed by two more chocolate biscuits.

In fact a whole packet of chocolate biscuits.

And as he finished the last biscuit, he heard a knocking sound.

It was coming from the oven.

"How odd," he thought to himself and he opened
the oven door.

And to his great surprise, out jumped his gingerbread man who
ran round the kitchen crying:

"Run, run as fast as you can!
You can't catch me, I'm the Gingerbread Man!"

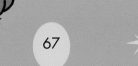

The Gingerbread Man ran out of the door and down the garden path.

Mr Greedy gave chase, but the Gingerbread Man was right. Mr Greedy couldn't catch him, and the Gingerbread Man was soon out of sight.

The Gingerbread Man ran up a hill and at the top he passed Mr Bump fetching water from a well.

"Run, run as fast as you can!
You can't catch me, I'm the Gingerbread Man!"

Mr Bump gave chase, but …

Oops!

Mr Bump tripped over his pail of water and rolled all the way down the hill and bumped his head.

The Gingerbread Man ran on.

He ran past Mr Lazy, asleep in his hammock.

"Run, run as fast as you can!
You can't catch me, I'm the Gingerbread Man!"

Mr Lazy opened an eye.

"You're not wrong," he said and he went back to sleep.

On ran the Gingerbread Man.

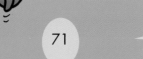

He ran past Little Miss Late.

*"Run, run as fast as you can!
You can't catch me, I'm the Gingerbread Man!"*

Little Miss Late took up the chase, but the Gingerbread Man
was too fast.

"Oh dear. I can't even catch a bus, let alone
the Gingerbread Man," sighed Little Miss Late.

Nobody could catch the Gingerbread Man.

Mr Slow was too slow.

 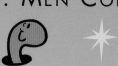 

Mr Muddle got in a muddle and ran the wrong way.

Even Mr Tickle's extraordinarily long arms were not long
enough to catch the Gingerbread Man.

  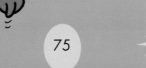 

"Nobody can catch me," boasted the Gingerbread Man, and he was so pleased with himself that he decided to lie down for a rest.

And he fell fast asleep.

"Caught you," said a voice, and a big pink hand picked up the Gingerbread Man.

"Slow and steady wins the race," continued Mr Greedy.

Mr Greedy took a big bite of the Gingerbread Man.

"Oh dear!" cried the Gingerbread Man. "I'm a quarter gone!"

Mr Greedy took another bite.

"Oh dear! Now I'm half gone!"

And another bite.

"Oh dear! I'm three quarters gone!"

And then one last bite.

"Oh dear," said Mr Greedy. "Now it's all gone …"

"… and I'm still hungry!"

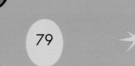

MR. STRONG
and the Ogre

Roger Hargreaves

Mr Strong is the strongest person in the World.
He is so strong he can balance an elephant on one finger.

But quite recently, it looked as though Mr Strong might have
met his match.

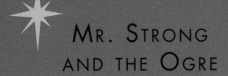

One day, Mr Strong met Little Miss Tiny on his way home from the shops. Little Miss Tiny was crying.

"What ever is the matter?" asked Mr Strong.

Little Miss Tiny told him. She had been walking back to her house, carrying a lollipop over her shoulder when a huge, ugly Ogre had leapt out from behind a bush blocking her path.

"Gimme yer lollipop!" the Ogre had demanded.

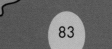

Poor Little Miss Tiny had no choice, but to give the Ogre her lollipop. Mr Strong was appalled.

"It is not far to my house," he said.
"I'll make you a cup of tea and we can work out what is to be done."

With Little Miss Tiny sitting on his shoulder, Mr Strong continued on his way.

Just around the corner, they came upon Mr Rush sitting at the side of the road, looking very shaken.

"What ever is wrong?" asked Mr Strong.

Mr Rush explained. He had been driving along the road when an enormous, brute of an Ogre had loomed up in the middle of the lane.

"Gimme yer car!" the Ogre had demanded.

Poor Mr Rush had no choice but to hand over his car and watch helplessly as the Ogre drove away in it.

Mr Strong suggested that Mr Rush join him and Little Miss Tiny for tea.

They had walked the last half a mile to Mr Strong's house when they met a very upset and indignant Mr Uppity.

This time Mr Strong had a very good idea what the matter was.

  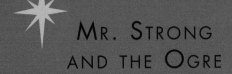  

Mr Uppity had been on his way to the bank to count his money when a huge, horrible Ogre had stepped out from behind a tree forcing Mr Uppity to stop.

"Gimme yer hat!" the Ogre had roared.

Poor Mr Uppity had no choice but to give the Ogre his hat. Which, not surprisingly, was far too small for the Ogre.

"I've heard enough!" announced Mr Strong. "Go inside and make yourselves some tea. I'm off to find this Ogre. I shan't be long."

Mr Strong had a pretty good idea where he might find the Ogre. Behind his garden, on the other side of the hill, there was a cave in the woods. Sure enough, this was where Mr Strong found the Ogre, lounging in the entrance to the cave, eating Little Miss Tiny's lollipop.

The only trouble was, there was not one Ogre, but three!
They were brothers.

The Ogres slowly raised themself to their full, menacing height.
Undaunted, Mr Strong marched up to the Ogres and introduced
himself.

"Strong! Yer don't know the meaning of strong. Just look at yer!"
mocked the biggest Ogre.

"If I prove I am stronger than the three of you, will you apologise
to my friends and promise to stop bullying?" asked Mr Strong.

"Stronger than the three of us!" boomed the biggest Ogre. "Even my little brother is stronger than you!"

"Can he lift this?" asked Mr Strong, raising a large rock above his head.

"Easy peasy," said the smallest Ogre.

Mr Strong passed the largest rock to the smallest Ogre, but it was too heavy for him and the Ogre dropped it on his toe.

"OWWW!" he bellowed in pain.

"Out of the way, titch," snarled the middle Ogre, pushing the youngest Ogre out of his way.

"I bet yer too weak to pick that up," he taunted, pointing at a huge slab of stone.

Mr Strong smiled and lifted it effortlessly.

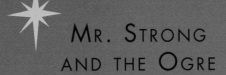

"Your turn," said Mr Strong.

The middle Ogre tried with all his might to lift the slab of stone. He raised one end three inches off the ground before he dropped it, trapping his fingers underneath.

"OWWW!" roared the middle Ogre in pain.

 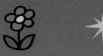

"Let me 'ave a go!" thundered the third Ogre, who was possibly the least clever of the three, but by far the largest.

With an enormous effort, the biggest Ogre lifted the stone slab above his head.

"Beat that," he grunted through gritted teeth.

But then his knees began to wobble, his legs started to tremble, his arms buckled and the rock came down on his head, knocking him out cold!

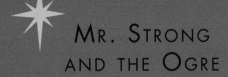

Mr Strong picked up the biggest Ogre as if he weighed no more than a feather and carried him, with the other two brothers following behind, over the hill, back to his house where he set him down in front of his three friends.

"Now we have got all that nonsense out of the way," said Mr Strong, "I think it is time you said sorry."

"We're sorry," mumbled the three Ogres in unison.

"We can't hear you," said Mr Strong.

"We're very sorry," said the Ogre brothers more clearly.

"Now that's done we can all have some tea," announced Mr Strong.

Which they did.

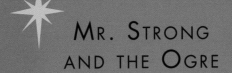

Although the Ogres did not stay long,
as tea parties are not really their thing.

MR. HAPPY
and the Wizard

Roger Hargreaves

Mr Happy goes to the Town Library every Saturday morning.

He went there last Saturday.

And he went there this Saturday.

He was looking along the shelves for a book to read when a very large and rather battered red volume caught his eye.

He pulled it out and looked at the spine.

It read, 'SPELL BOOK'.

He was about to return it to its place when a voice suddenly said, "Don't you dare! I've been stuck on that shelf for a week!"

Mr Happy dropped the book in surprise.

"Ow!" said the book, for it was the book that had spoken.

There was a face on the cover – nose, eyes, mouth, everything!

Mr Happy was too amazed to speak.

"Oooh," wheezed the book. "You get terribly cramped if you're wedged on a shelf for too long. Now then, what's your name?"

"Mr Happy," said Mr Happy, finding his voice at last.

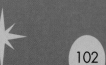

"Hello, I'm a spell book," said the book. "I belong to a Wizard, but the silly, absent-minded fool left me here. Look! He even forgot his hat! When I was asleep someone tidied me away up on that shelf. I need a lift home. Will you help me?"

Mr Happy agreed, and wearing the Wizard's hat, with the spell book under his arm, he set off through the countryside.

Mr Happy felt just like a real Wizard!

Along the way they met Mr Forgetful who was standing beside a phone box muttering to himself.

"Do you have any spells in there that could help Mr Forgetful's memory?" Mr Happy asked the spell book.

"Of course," said the spell book, and opened on the right page.

Mr Happy read out the spell and watched Mr Forgetful.

"I remember!" cried Mr Forgetful. "I've got to ring Mr
Chatterbox … and I forgot to lock my house … oh no,
I forgot to turn off my bath … and I didn't post that letter …
and I haven't bought any milk … and I must water
the plants and …"

Mr Forgetful was frantically running around in circles by this
point, worrying about all the things he had forgotten.

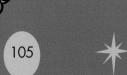

"Oh dear! Do you have any spells to make people forget things?" Mr Happy said to the book.

The spell book opened at a different page and as soon as Mr Happy said the spell, Mr Forgetful looked a lot happier.

Mr Happy and the spell book continued on their way.

They heard somebody talking to himself around a bend in the road.

"If I cross over now then I might get run over, but if I don't cross over then how will I get to the other side? Oh dear, oh dear."

It was Mr Worry.

Mr Happy looked down at the spell book.

"Do you want to know if I have any spells to stop people worrying?" guessed the spell book, and opened to the right page.

Mr Happy read out the spell.

   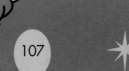 

"I don't care!" shouted Mr Worry, suddenly. "Hee! Hee! I'm worry free! I'll just close my eyes and step out into the …"

CRASH! He walked straight into Mr Bump on his bicycle.

"Maybe worrying is safer after all," said Mr Happy, and the spell book flicked over a couple of pages to the spell that would return Mr Worry to normal.

It was a very long walk to the Wizard's house. In the middle of the afternoon Mr Happy caught up with a hot and tired Mr Small.

"How about a spell for longer legs?" suggested Mr Happy.

"Coming right up," replied the spell book.

Mr Small's legs grew and grew.

He strode off down the road at a terrific pace, until he reached a tree and banged his head on a branch. The same thing happened on the second tree he came to. And on the trees all the way down the road.

BANG! OUCH!
BANG! OUCH!
BANG! OUCH!

Mr Happy winced.

"Shorter legs?" asked the spell book.

Mr Happy nodded.

By the evening they came to a wood.

"We're nearly there now," said the spell book happily.

Finally they reached a cottage in a clearing.

The Wizard opened the door. He was overjoyed.

"My spell book and my hat! I've been looking high and low for them for so long that I'd nearly given up hope! Thank you!"

He invited Mr Happy in for supper.

A Wizard's supper.

They ate Everything Pie.

The pie changed as they ate, so every mouthful tasted different!

After supper was finished and the washing-up spell had done its work, the Wizard turned to Mr Happy.

"There must be something I can do for you. Choose any spell you wish. Choose anything you want!"

  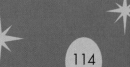 

Mr Happy smiled. "After seeing what spells can do,
I think I'm happy as I am!" he laughed.

MR. FUNNY
and the Magic Lamp

Roger Hargreaves

Mr Funny lives in a teapot.

A teapot house.

How ridiculous I hear you say, but it suited Mr Funny right down to its spout.

Now, one day last spring, Mr Funny discovered an old trunk in his attic, which is under the lid.

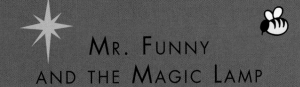

And in the trunk he found a carpet.

A carpet that gave him a surprise.

For it was a magic carpet. A magic flying carpet.

Mr Funny was very excited.

There and then he decided to go on a trip to see where the magic carpet would take him.

So on that spring morning he set off on an adventure.

Mr Funny flew over Lazyland, where he woke up
Mr Lazy with a very loud raspberry and a funny face.

Mr Lazy laughed so much he fell out of bed.

 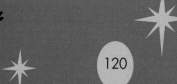  

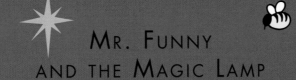

Mr Funny and his magic carpet flew over Fatland, where Mr Funny made Mr Skinny laugh.

He laughed so much he tripped over a daisy and dropped the breadcrumb he was carrying for his picnic lunch.

And they flew over Coldland, where Mr Funny made Mr Sneeze laugh.

He laughed so much that he stopped sneezing!

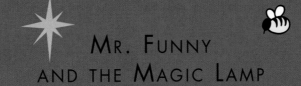

The magic carpet flew on and on.

They flew over mountains and valleys and over the sea.

Finally, they arrived in a desert.

But there was nobody there. Nobody to laugh at Mr Funny's funny faces.

Then, just as he was about to leave, Mr Funny saw something half buried in the sand. It was a lamp.

"What a grubby old lamp," he said to himself and he gave it a rub.

Suddenly, with a clap of thunder and in a cloud of smoke,
a genie appeared in front of Mr Funny.

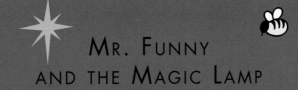

Which was all very exciting, but what Mr Funny noticed most of all was how miserable the genie looked.

Mr Funny had never seen anyone look so unhappy.

"Master," said the genie, glumly, "I am the Genie of the Lamp and I appear before you to grant you three wishes."

To the genie's surprise, Mr Funny pulled one of his famous funny faces.

But the genie did not laugh.

He did not chuckle.

He did not even smile.

Not a flicker.

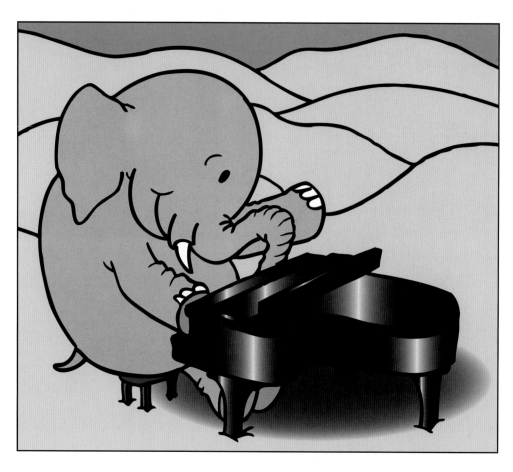

"Oh dear," said Mr Funny. It was going to take a bit more than a funny face to cheer up this genie.

And then he had a thought.

"For my first wish, I wish for a piano-playing elephant."

"As you command, Master," said the genie, and then before you could say 'broken piano stool' a piano-playing elephant appeared before them.

Mr Funny roared with laughter.

It was hilarious!

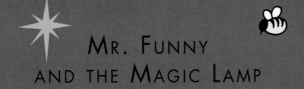

But it was not funny enough to make the genie laugh.

He looked just as glum as before.

Mr Funny had another thought.

"For my second wish, I wish for a mouse."

And before you could say 'squeak' a mouse appeared.

And as Mr Funny and you probably know, great big elephants are frightened of teeny tiny mice.

The elephant trumpeted in fear and jumped on top of the piano, which broke under the elephant's weight.

Mr Funny laughed with delight.

"Now, that was funny," chuckled Mr Funny.

"Not really," said the genie, who looked just as unhappy as before.

"You are a gloomy fellow," said Mr Funny.

"You would be too," said the genie, "if you had to live in that lamp!"

"It must be a tight squeeze," admitted Mr Funny.

"You can say that again," grumbled the genie. "There's no room even to cough living in a lamp."

"I live in a teapot. A very comfortable teapot, mind you,"
said Mr Funny, and then yet another thought struck him.

"For my third wish, I wish your lamp was a house."

And before you could say 'bring me a builder'
the Genie's lamp had turned into a house!

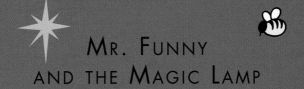

The genie smiled.

Only a flicker of a smile, but at least a smile.

"That's more like it," said Mr Funny. "Now, how am I going to get this elephant back home? I know! I wish …"

"I'm sorry," interrupted the genie. "You've used up your three wishes."

So Mr Funny and the elephant had to squeeze on to the magic carpet for their ride home. It was quite a sight.

Rather funny, in fact.

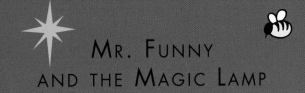

So funny, the genie roared with laughter!

MR. MEN
Sports Day

Roger Hargreaves

Have you ever been to Nonsenseland?

In Nonsenseland, the grass is blue and the trees are red.
And all the cars have square wheels.

Why?

Easy! So they don't roll away when they are parked on a hill.

I know, what nonsense!

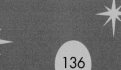 

And in Nonsenseland they hold a sports day every summer.

Nothing silly about that I hear you say.

Well, you'll just have to wait and see.

This year, the preparations for the sports day started two weeks before the event and, it being Nonsenseland, things happened somewhat differently to how you would have expected.

Little Miss Scatterbrain got the sports field ready.

Mr Dizzy marked out the track for the races.

And Mr Nonsense got the finishing line ready.

A very silly-looking finishing line!

The day of the Nonsenseland Sports Day dawned to a great deal of excitement. All the Mr Men were there, and no one was more excited than Mr Rush who was at the sports day for the very first time.

He couldn't wait for the last event of the day.

The 100 metre sprint.

But for the first time in his life he did wait.

There were lots of other events to watch first.

However, as each one came and went, Mr Rush became more and more confused.

The high jump had become the low jump and was won by Mr Small.

And the long jump was the short jump. Won by Little Miss Tiny.

Throwing the hammer became throwing the jelly. Won by Mr Strong, whose jelly went a bit further than he intended it to!

Little Miss Naughty was leading all the way in the sack race.

But Mr Nosey won it by a nose.

For the swimming gala, Mr Silly had filled the swimming pool with custard!

Mr Tickle won by a hand … on the end of his extraordinarily long arm.

And the egg and spoon race became the raw egg and teaspoon race.

Much trickier … and a lot messier!

Finally, it was time for the 100 metre sprint.

Mr Rush and all the other runners took their places at the starting line. The starting pistol fired, Mr Rush shot down the track and before you could say "six speedy sausages!" he had crossed the finish line.

"I've won!" cried Mr Rush.

Everyone gathered round for the prize presentation.

Mr Rush could not wait to hear the announcement.

The King of Nonsenseland stood up on stage.

"In third place," he said, "is Mr Silly for the silliest running shoes ever!"

"In second place," he continued, "is Little Miss Dotty for the silliest running outfit."

"And in first place, for by far the silliest 100 metre sprint, is Mr Slow!"

"But … but … but Mr Slow didn't even run! Look, he hasn't finished yet!" cried Mr Rush, who could not believe what he'd just heard.

"Exactly," said the King. "He walked. What could be sillier than entering a running race and then not running! And here he comes now!"

Poor Mr Rush hadn't realised that the event was called the 'silliest' 100 metre sprint.

"But … but that's nonsense," said Mr Rush.

"Exactly," said Mr Slow. "Complete nonsense."

And he stepped forward to collect his cup.

A tea cup!

MR.
NOISY
and the Giant

Roger Hargreaves

Mr Noisy is the noisiest person you will ever meet.

His voice is so loud it can shake the birds from the trees.

It can even shake the birds from the trees across the other side of the world!

Last month, Mr Noisy decided to call his friend Mr Quiet, who lives many, many hills away.

But Mr Noisy does not have a telephone. He does not need one.

Do you know what he does when he wants to speak to someone?

He goes out of his front door and shouts!

When Mr Quiet heard Mr Noisy's booming voice, he nearly jumped out of his chair.

Mr Noisy's loud voice scares most people.

When Mr Jelly met Mr Noisy, he was so frightened that he ran straight home and stayed under his bed for a week.

And when Mr Noisy said hello to Little Miss Splendid, he made her hair stand on end.

But Mr Noisy is not the only person with a huge voice.

There is one other person who is just as loud as Mr Noisy.

  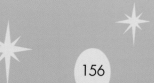  

That person is a Giant.

A Giant who lives surprisingly close to where you live, but even closer to Mr Noisy.

The Giant is enormous.

His feet are the size of sofas.

He is so tall that he has to bend down to look into Mr Tall's bedroom window.

But by far the biggest thing about the Giant is his voice.

And that is the Giant's biggest problem in life.

Whenever he tries to talk to anyone, they run away.

His huge, loud, booming, thunderous voice terrifies everybody.

Just one "HELLO!" is enough to send them running for the hills.

And so the Giant is a very sad and lonely Giant.

One hot summer's day, the Giant was resting on the river bank, cooling his feet in the water, when he heard footsteps.

Very loud, thumping footsteps.

And the very loud, thumping footsteps were accompanied by whistling.

Whistling as loudly as a train whistle.

The Giant was very excited.

That must be another Giant, he thought to himself.

Another Giant who could be my friend.

The Giant peered over the hill. But on the other side of the hill, he did not see another Giant.

I am sure you can guess who he saw instead.

That's right!

It was Mr Noisy!

"HELLO!" boomed the Giant, in his quietest voice.

But because Mr Noisy is so used to loud noises he did not run away like anyone else would have.

"HELLO!" he boomed back, in a voice as loud as the Giant's.

In no time at all, the Giant and Mr Noisy were chatting.

The loudest chat in the world!

The Giant so enjoyed their chat that he invited Mr Noisy to tea.

And to the Giant's delight, Mr Noisy accepted his invitation.

The Giant talked and talked and talked, while
Mr Noisy sat sipping tea out of the Giant's thimble.

They talked right through the afternoon and into the evening.

They talked so late that Mr Noisy was invited to stay the night.

In the Giant's extraordinarily large spare room.

In the Giant's extraordinarily large spare bed.

The two of them snored so loudly that they very nearly shook the roof off the house!

The next morning, while having a swim in the Giant's extraordinarily large bath, Mr Noisy had an idea.

He explained his idea to the Giant over breakfast.

"I HAVE A FRIEND CALLED MR QUIET," boomed Mr Noisy,
"AND HE USED TO LIVE IN A PLACE CALLED LOUDLAND.
I THINK THAT YOU AND I SHOULD GO ON HOLIDAY
TO LOUDLAND!"

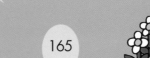

"WHAT A GREAT IDEA!" thundered the Giant.

And so off they went.

And it was perfect.

Because, you see, in Loudland everything and everybody is loud.

Extremely loud.

Even the worms are loud in Loudland.

Mr Noisy and the Giant could be as loud as they liked.

They fitted in very well.

Except for one thing.

One very LARGE thing.

The Giant could not fit into his hotel bed!

MR. BIRTHDAY

Roger Hargreaves

The very best thing about birthdays, as far as Mr Birthday is concerned, is birthday parties.

Cards are nice, presents are good, but parties are great.

Mr Birthday likes birthday parties so much that he is never without his party hat!

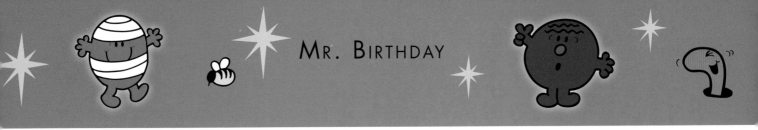

And Mr Birthday is very good at organising birthday parties. He likes to make sure that everyone he knows has a party on their birthday.

In just the last three weeks, he has organised a party with two cakes for Mr Greedy.

One cake for all the guests and one for Mr Greedy!

A party with silly hats for Mr Silly because …

… Mr Silly is silly!

And a party with no balloons for Mr Jelly because Mr Jelly is scared of balloons …

… in case they go POP!

This week, Mr Birthday organised a very happy birthday party for Mr Happy.

He invited all of Mr Happy's friends, including Little Miss Sunshine, Mr Funny, Little Miss Lucky and Mr Bump.

Mr Birthday put up lots of balloons and a big banner saying "Happy Birthday, Mr Happy!"

And he organised fun party games for everyone to play.

 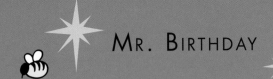

Little Miss Lucky won pass the parcel.

And then she won pin the tail on the donkey.

She is not called Little Miss Lucky for nothing!

It was difficult to know who won musical chairs because
Mr Bump kept knocking over the chairs.

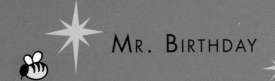

After the party games, Mr Birthday brought in a huge birthday cake. Mr Happy smiled an extra wide smile and blew out all the candles in one go!

Then they all ate a feast of birthday cake, jam sandwiches, jelly and ice-cream.

Everyone had a wonderful time.

When the party had finished, Mr Happy thanked Mr Birthday.

"We mustn't forget that extra special birthday next week,"
added Mr Happy with a wink, as he said goodbye.

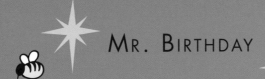

Mr Birthday racked his brains as he walked home.

"I wonder whose birthday Mr Happy was talking about," he puzzled.

But try as he might, no one came to mind.

He looked in his diary when he reached home, but there was no one's birthday written in for the next week.

"Mr Happy must have got it wrong," he reassured himself as he got into bed.

But the next day, Mr Birthday kept overhearing things that seemed to suggest there really was a very important birthday coming up.

He passed Mr Worry in the street.

"Oh my! Oh gosh! What ever am I going to buy as a present for next week?" muttered Mr Worry to himself. "What a worry!"

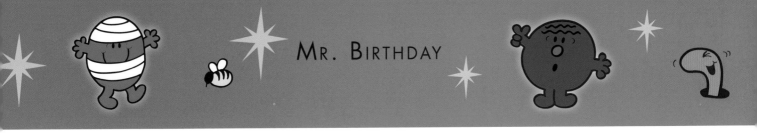

He overheard Mr Forgetful who was repeating, "I must not forget the party next week, I must not forget the party next week, I must not forget the party next week," over and over to himself.

"I must not forget the …" he said and stopped mid-sentence. Then he looked at his hand, "… the party! I must not forget the party next week."

Poor Mr Birthday was distraught. How could there be a birthday, and a birthday party, he knew nothing about?

The following day, he decided that he would just have to go and ask Mr Happy.

Mr Happy smiled an even wider smile than usual when Mr Birthday admitted that he did not have a clue whose birthday they were all talking about.

"If you come back at 3 o'clock on Tuesday then I will tell you whose birthday it is," said Mr Happy.

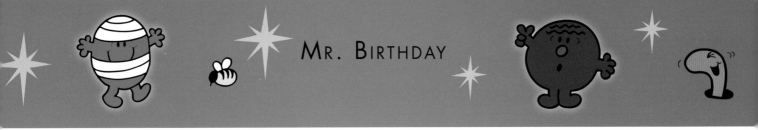

By Tuesday, Mr Birthday was very, very curious.

Have you guessed whose birthday it is yet?

Mr Birthday turned up at Mr Happy's house at 3 o'clock on the dot.

"You have got to tell me now!" burst out Mr Birthday, when Mr Happy opened the door.

"With pleasure," grinned Mr Happy. "It is …"

"… your birthday!"

"Happy birthday, Mr Birthday!"
cried all of Mr Birthday's friends.

Mr Birthday blushed. "How silly of me!" he said.

MR. BUMP
and the Knight

Roger Hargreaves

Mr Bump was thoroughly fed up. It did not seem to matter what he did, he always ended up getting bumped and bruised or scraped and scratched.

So, you can imagine how hard it was for him to find a job.

He had tried working at the baker's, but he had burnt his fingers on the bread oven.

OUCH!

He had tried being a bricklayer, but he had dropped a brick
on his foot.

THUD!

OUCH!

He had even tried working at the pillow factory.

Who could hurt themselves in a pillow factory?

Mr Bump, of course!

He got a feather in his eye!

OUCH!

Every day it was bandage this and bandage that.
Poor Mr Bump was very fed up.

Then one day, while Mr Bump was walking in the woods behind his house, he met someone who gave him a wonderful idea.

The perfect idea for a new job.

That someone was a Knight in shining armour, riding by on his horse.

Now, it was not the thought of the excitement and adventure of being a Knight that caught Mr Bump's imagination, nor was it the idea of the fame and fortune he might win. No, it was the Knight's solid, metal armour that caught his eye.

Shining armour that protected the Knight from bumps and bruises, scrapes and scratches.

"If I wore armour like that," thought Mr Bump to himself, "I would never need to worry about bumping myself again. I shall become a Knight."

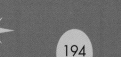

Early the next morning, Mr Bump rushed to the blacksmith's to buy himself a suit of armour.

The blacksmith had to put the armour on very carefully to avoid Mr Bump's bruises, but when he had it on, Mr Bump looked at his reflection in the mirror and smiled.

Mr Bump then bought a book called 'Knights, All You Need to Know'.

"Now," said Mr Bump, opening the book, "what do Knights do?"

He read a whole chapter about jousting. Then he went out and bought a horse and a lance and went to a local jousting tournament.

However, Mr Bump quickly found out that he was not very good at jousting. Every time he sat on his horse he fell off.

CRASH!

The other Knights thought it was hilarious.

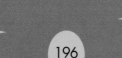

That evening, Mr Bump opened his book and read a chapter called 'Saving Damsels in Distress'.

The next day, he set off, on foot, to find a damsel in need of saving.

Fortunately, because it was very awkward walking in a suit of armour, Mr Bump found one near his house.

A damsel locked in a very tall tower.

"Will you save me, Sir Knight?" cried the Damsel.

"I will!" Mr Bump called back.

The Damsel let down a ladder woven from her long, fine hair.

But try as hard as he might, Mr Bump could not climb the ladder.

He kept falling off at every attempt.

BANG! CRASH! CLUNK!

Feeling rather sorry for himself, and even more sorry for the Damsel, Mr Bump trudged off home.

The next chapter in the book was entitled 'Slaying Dragons'.

"That's the one for me!" cried Mr Bump.

The following day, Mr Bump bought a sword and shield and went in search of a dragon. There were not any near by, so he caught the bus.

The dragon was asleep on the top of a steep hill.

It took Mr Bump a lot of huffing and puffing to climb to the top.

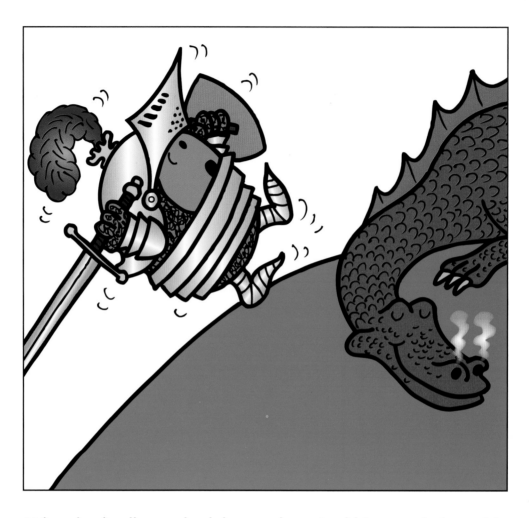

When he finally reached the top, he raised his sword above his head to slay the dragon, but the weight of the sword tipped Mr Bump off balance.

With a great CRASHING and CLATTERING of armour, he rolled all the way down the hill.

IIt was a very sad Mr Bump who got back home later that day.

He had to face the fact that he was not cut out to be a Knight.

He went up to his bedroom and took off his armour.

And then he noticed something quite remarkable.

When he glimpsed himself in the mirror, it was a very different Mr Bump looking back at him

A Mr Bump without a bandage or a plaster in sight.

A Mr Bump without a bump or a bruise.

Mr Bump smiled.

And then he laughed …

… and then he fell over backwards and bumped
his head on the bed!

MR. MEN
A White Christmas

Roger Hargreaves

Father Christmas, as you might imagine, is very busy just before Christmas. And one of the jobs that keeps him busy is reading everyone's Christmas letters.

Last year, he received a letter from a little boy in Australia who had a very special wish. He wished for a white Christmas.

Now, as you might or might not know, it is very hot at Christmas time in Australia. And because it is very hot at Christmas, it never snows.

"Hmm," said Father Christmas to himself. "Now, who would be the best person to help me with this wish?"

And so it was that Mr Snow received a visit from Father Christmas.

"Hello, Mr Snow," said Father Christmas. "I have a job for you. A little boy in Australia called Ben has asked for a white Christmas. Do you think you can make his wish come true?"

"I think I know just the person who can," said Mr Snow, after a moment's thought.

"Excellent!" said Father Christmas. "You can borrow my sleigh. It's a rather long walk to Australia!"

Mr Snow packed his suitcase and set off for Australia.

On the way he picked up a very good friend of his, Little Miss Magic. It took them no time at all to get to Australia in Father Christmas's sleigh.

Ben was very excited when he saw Mr Snow and Little Miss Magic standing on his doorstep.

"Hello, Ben," said Little Miss Magic. "We're here to make your wish come true."

"I think we need to hurry up," said Mr Snow. "I'm starting to melt!"

So Little Miss Magic muttered some very magic words and suddenly the temperature dropped, huge grey clouds rolled over the horizon, and it began to snow.

Ben could not believe his eyes.

It snowed.

And it snowed.

Everywhere was covered in a thick blanket of fluffy, white snow.

Ben ran inside his house and put on all his jumpers.

"Would you like to come for a ride in Father Christmas's flying sleigh?" asked Mr Snow.

"Yes please!" said Ben.

They climbed aboard and Mr Snow took off.

Ben looked in wonder at the snowy landscape below them.

But everywhere they went Ben began to notice the same thing.

The kangaroos, standing in the snowy outback, did
not look very happy.

The crocodiles in the icy river did not look very happy.

And everyone on the snowy beach did not look very happy.

They looked very unhappy and very cold.

"Oh dear," sighed Ben. "I don't think anyone else wants the snow as much as I do. I think you'd better make it all go away."

So Little Miss Magic muttered some more very magic words and before you could say, "Hey Presto" the clouds had rolled away and the sun came out and melted all the snow.

Ben looked sadly at the puddles at his feet. And it was then that Mr Snow had an idea. "Why don't we fly to places where people do like snow?"

"Can we?" cried Ben.

"We certainly can," said Little Miss Magic.

And so they did just that.

They flew to Coldland and went sledging with Mr Sneeze.

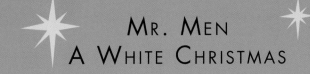

Then they visited Mr Bump and went ice skating.

"Do you know where they have more snow than anywhere else?" Mr Snow asked.

"Where?" asked Ben.

"At the North Pole!" said Mr Snow.

"That's where Father Christmas lives!" cried Ben.

"Indeed it is," said Mr Snow.

And that is how a little boy from Australia found himself at the North Pole in …

… a snowball fight with Mr Snow, Little Miss Christmas, Mr Christmas and Father Christmas!

And what a snowball fight it was!

"I'm sorry you didn't get to have a white Christmas in Australia," laughed Mr Snow, as his snowball hit Father Christmas's chest.

"But at least you did get to see one white Christmas …"

"… a white Father Christmas! We've turned him into a snowman!"